P9-AFF-285

Dear Parents:

Congratulations! Your child is taking the first steps on an exciting journey. The destination? Independent reading!

STEP INTO READING® will help your child get there. The program offers five steps to reading success. Each step includes fun stories and colorful art or photographs. In addition to original fiction and books with favorite characters, there are Step into Reading Non-Fiction Readers, Phonics Readers and Boxed Sets, Sticker Readers, and Comic Readers—a complete literacy program with something to interest every child.

Learning to Read, Step by Step!

Ready to Read **Preschool–Kindergarten**
• big type and easy words • rhyme and rhythm • picture clues
For children who know the alphabet and are eager to begin reading.

Reading with Help **Preschool–Grade 1**
• basic vocabulary • short sentences • simple stories
For children who recognize familiar words and sound out new words with help.

Reading on Your Own **Grades 1–3**
• engaging characters • easy-to-follow plots • popular topics
For children who are ready to read on their own.

Reading Paragraphs **Grades 2–3**
• challenging vocabulary • short paragraphs • exciting stories
For newly independent readers who read simple sentences with confidence.

Ready for Chapters **Grades 2–4**
• chapters • longer paragraphs • full-color art
For children who want to take the plunge into chapter books but still like colorful pictures.

STEP INTO READING® is designed to give every child a successful reading experience. The grade levels are only guides; children will progress through the steps at their own speed, developing confidence in their reading.

Remember, a lifetime love of reading starts with a single step!

Special thanks to Ryan Ferguson, Kristine Lombardi, Debra Mostow Zakarin, Stuart Smith, Sammie Suchland, Nicole Corse, Charnita Belcher, Julia Phelps, Julia Pistor, Hillary Powell, Garrett Sander, Kris Fogel, Lauren Rose, Sarah Serata, Renevee Romero, and Snowball Studios

www.barbie.com
Published in the United States by Random House Children's Books, a division of Penguin Random House LLC, 1745 Broadway, New York, NY 10019, and in Canada by Penguin Random House Canada Limited, Toronto.

Visit us on the Web!
StepIntoReading.com
randomhousekids.com

Educators and librarians, for a variety of teaching tools, visit us at RHTeachersLibrarians.com

ISBN 978-1-5247-1638-7 (trade) — ISBN 978-1-5247-1639-4 (lib. bdg.)

Printed in the United States of America
10 9 8 7 6 5 4 3 2 1

STEP 2 STEP INTO READING® READING WITH HELP

Barbie™ Dreamtopia

The Best Birthday

Adapted by Mary Man-Kong

Based on the original story
by Devra Newberger Speregen

Illustrated by Federica Salfo,
Francesco Legramandi, and Charles Pickens

Random House New York

It is the day before
Chelsea's birthday.
Everyone is
so excited.

Jace cannot go to
Chelsea's party.
Chelsea will
miss him.

Chelsea does not know
what to wish for
on her birthday.
Otto wants to
take her wish.

That night,
Chelsea worries that Otto
will take her wish.

Chelsea dreams of sailing
to the magical world
of Dreamtopia.

In Wispy Forest,
Chelsea's hair turns
into a cupcake.
Barbie the Forest Princess
asks what Chelsea wishes
for her birthday.

Chelsea still
does not know.

The Notto Prince plays
a trick on Chelsea.
He puts a Mople
in her hair.

Chelsea wishes he would leave her alone. The Notto Prince disappears!

Chelsea tells Barbie the Rainbow Princess that she did not want to wish the Notto Prince away.

Barbie brings
back the Notto Prince.
Chelsea did not want that
to be her wish either.

The Rainbow Princess
creates a cake.
Chelsea can make
another wish.

The Notto Prince tries to take her wish! Chelsea wishes he would go away again.

Chelsea's wish
comes true.
The Notto Prince
flies away.

Barbie the Sugar Spun
Fairy asks Chelsea
what she wants
for her birthday.

Chelsea knows
what to wish for now.
She wishes
to spend her birthday
with all her friends.

The Notto Prince appears!

They become friends.

Chelsea sees her friends.
They are there
for her surprise party!

At home,

Jace comes to the party.

Chelsea's wish comes true!

It is the best birthday!